Copyright © 2016 by Mattel, Inc. All rights reserved.
MONSTER HIGH and associated trademarks are owned by and used under license from Mattel, Inc.

Little, Brown and Company

Hachette Book Group
1290 Avenue of the Americas, New York, NY 10104
Visit us at lb-kids.com

Little, Brown and Company is a division of Hachette Book Group, Inc.
The Little, Brown name and logo are trademarks of Hachette Book Group, Inc.

The publisher is not responsible for websites (or their content) that are not owned by the publisher.

First Edition: September 2016

Library of Congress Control Number: 2016938027

ISBN 978-0-316-39460-4

10 9 8 7 6 5 4 3 2

LSC-C

Printed in the United States of America

WELCOME TO MONSTER HIGH

The Junior Novel

ADAPTED BY
Perdita Finn

BASED ON THE SCREENPLAY WRITTEN BY
**Dana Starfield and
Shane Amsterdam**

LITTLE, BROWN AND COMPANY
New York   Boston

Chapter 1

Midnight at Monster High

Alarm clocks were ringing, sleepy students were yawning, and another normal night at Monster High was about to begin. But as Draculaura always says, "*Normal* is relative."

The alarm clock was shaped like a skull. The hand that hit the snooze button wasn't a hand at all. It was a tentacle! A beastie named Woolee staggered into her bathroom to brush her tusks with a giant kitchen broom. Elsewhere, muddy water sprayed out of a rusty showerhead. A swamp monster happily scrubbed the thorny vines of his hair.

Claws and flippers were opening re-odorant,

checking lipstick, and unscrewing tubes of hair gloop. It was midnight. School was about to begin.

"Normal is about how you feel," Draculaura explained. "Not how you look or what you do."

A skeleton, Bonesy, polished his skull with a buffer in front of the mirror. His brother, Skelly, put on a pair of cool shades. Too bad he didn't have ears to hold them in place; they slipped right off his earless head.

"Normal is different for everyone," Draculaura added. She looked at the brightly colored outfit she had laid out on her bed. It didn't seem quite right. What should she wear today? She looked in her closet.

Her white miniskirt with the black netting. Her black shirt. Her pink vest. That was the look she was going for. A little Goth. A little pretty. And *all* vampire.

Monsters were sleepily headed to the Creepateria for breakfast. A piece of toast popped out of the ghoaster. An enormous mountain of cereal was disappearing from a bowl. Behind it was a gobbling glob of purple goblin. Gob munched spoonful after spoonful of his breakfast, slurped the milk, and ate the spoon. He devoured the bowl and the cereal box. Everything sloshed around in his plump tummy, including the bowling ball and the cowboy hat he'd eaten earlier in the morning. He let out an enormous burp.

At other tables, monsters dug into their midnight meals—raw steaks and rotten apples, Jell-O and snow cones.

The school bell was ringing! Monsters of all kinds were hurrying through the forest to get to class on time. Bonesy had an enormous backpack hung around his shoulder blade. He caught up to Woolee. Ahead of them loomed the turrets and towers of Monster High. The moon was full. Fog hung low.

Draculaura knew that this must all seem very strange to the Normies. But to her—and a bunch of swamp things, werewolves, vampires, and mummies coming together—it was just Monday.

But how it came to be normal for Draculaura, and how she and her friend Frankie Stein brought monsters from all over the world together, is a kind of amazing story. And it all began one night not so very long ago...

Chapter 2

Fright Flight

A spider lowered himself on a thread from the gutter of a large run-down house with turrets and towers. Swinging back and forth like a superhero, he launched himself through an attic window. He landed right in Draculaura's bedroom. *Home again. What a relief.* He curled into a corner to take a nap.

Draculaura's room looked like any teenager's, any "normal" teenager's—except, that is, for the plush, satin-lined coffin where she slept. Still, everything else was normal. There were clothes in the closet and on the floor. There was a bulletin board with messages to herself. There were posters of her favorite pop stars, including teen idol Tash, the hit sensation sweeping the Normie nation.

Draculaura had her earbuds in; she was humming and dancing to a Tash song. She waved her hands. She lunged. She wiggled. She jumped. She pretended to sing. She didn't hear someone rapping at the window. The rapping grew louder and louder and more insistent.

Webby, her pet spider, couldn't sleep with all the noise. He swung down in front of Draculaura to get her attention. He pointed with one of his eight legs at the window.

"Draculaura!" someone was calling from outside.

Draculaura pulled out her earbuds. She opened the window. A vampire was hanging upside down and peeking in through the glass. It was her dad!

"Come on, Draculaura," he said impatiently. "Are you ready?"

"Hey, Dad," Draculaura answered. She was in no hurry at all. Until she remembered. She gulped visibly. "Oh, right. It's tonight." She took a deep breath. "I can do this."

Her father looked concerned. "Why don't we try this some other time? When you're more comfortable."

"I'm comfortable now, Dad," she said, rolling her eyes.

"I'm just saying…."

Determined, Draculaura climbed out of the window, perching on a ledge near her father.

"Now remember," advised her father, "you can never be too cautious. The outside world is a scary place filled with…*humans*!"

Draculaura giggled. "Oh no! Not the humans!" she said, pretending to be scared.

"This is no laughing matter!" Dracula scolded. Her father, still upside down, shook his head. "They may look innocent enough, but humans are one of the most dangerous species on earth."

"*Oooh,*" mocked Draculaura. "More dangerous than a swarm of killer robot bees?"

Her father was becoming angry. "I was about to make a very critical point."

"Stay away from humans." Draculaura sighed. How many times had she heard it before?

"*Stay. Away. From. Humans!*" exclaimed her

father, punctuating each word of his warning with a stern look. "It's essential that you never let one see you. They're just not ready to accept us, at least not yet. Promise me. Vamp's honor."

"Ugh!" Draculaura squeezed her eyes shut, concentrating. "I promise. Now, if you don't mind…"

Draculaura's eyes opened. She sprinted along the ledge and leaped into the air.

Poof!

Draculaura transformed herself into a bat! But something was the matter. Her wings were too tiny. Way too tiny. She was flapping them furiously, but they weren't big enough to support her. With a gentle thump, she landed on the flat roof of her house.

"Ugh." She was disappointed with herself. Flying was just so hard.

Her father hovered close. "Not all vampires get the bat transformation on their first try. Second time's the charm!"

No longer a bat, Draculaura psyched herself up for another go at it. She took several steps back on the roof. She geared herself up and exploded into a sprint, running as fast as she could. She leaped into the air.

Poof! She was a bat again. This time her wings held her. She fluttered. It seemed like she was going to swoop and soar.

But Draculaura was wobbling. She couldn't steer. She careened downward, hitting the sloping tiles of one of the turrets. She bounced, turning back into a ghoul. She bounced, turning back into a bat. Bat. Ghoul. Bat. Ghoul. Bounce, bounce, *OUCH!*

From the window of her bedroom, Webby watched. He winced.

"I'm all right. I got this," she said. But she didn't.

Draculaura tumbled down, down, down, finally landing in some overgrown bushes near the house. With twigs and leaves in her hair, she climbed back up the stairs to the roof. But she felt defeated. "I can't do this! It's impossible," she cried.

"Not impossible. Just challenging," encouraged her father. "Come on, let's try it together. One, two…"

Dracula lifted into the air effortlessly. With

a graceful turn, he transformed into a bat. He
fluttered over to Draculaura and nodded his head
supportively.

Just one more time. She could do this. Yes, she
could. Draculaura leaped up toward her father.
Poof! She was a bat.

Her wings were the right size. She was
echolocating. She could do this.

The two bats wafted through the night air
together.

"I did it!" exclaimed Draculaura.

"That's my ghoul," said Dracula proudly.

Together, the bats soared above Monster Hill.
Their silhouettes were dark against the moon.

They were gliding above the trees near Normie Town when a huge billboard caught Draculaura's eye. It was Tash! Draculaura's idol! Her favorite singer ever. The billboard was announcing her Flawless tour. Singing a Tash song to herself, Draculaura dove through the air happily.

Zonk!

Draculaura hadn't seen the telephone pole. She turned back into a ghoul as she fell through the air to the ground. Her father, still a bat, hovered beside her. "Drac, Drac, are you all right?"

Draculaura rubbed her head. "Yeah, fine, I think."

"One must never get distracted while flying," her father reminded her.

Draculaura jumped up and turned into a bat again. She and her father wafted past the billboard of Tash's beautiful, blond perfection.

"What were you thinking?" Dracula asked his daughter.

"Pop?" asked Draculaura. "Can I ask you something?" Without even waiting for an answer, she continued. "Okay, there's this amazing girl.

Tash. She's a big star and all. The Normal girls my age are obsessed with her—"

"Normal girls?" interrupted Dracula. "You mean *human* girls."

"Tash is totally, undeniably *creeptastic*!" Draculaura exclaimed. She couldn't keep it in anymore. She had to ask her father. She just had to. "Can I go to her concert? It's only, like, three towns over, and I'll be super careful. Please? Pretty please with cobwebs on top?"

Dracula hovered to a standstill in the air, thinking. "Drac, no," he said sadly. "I'm sorry. You know it's just too dangerous. Monsters don't belong in the human world."

Draculaura's wings beat furiously. She was upset. "But…please…I just…please," she begged.

Dracula sighed as he headed back toward their home. He wasn't going to fight with her. The answer was no.

Draculaura took one last lingering look at the billboard. "Then where *do* I belong?" she wondered out loud.

What good was it to know how to fly if she couldn't go anywhere? She sank down into a field of flowers. She turned back into a ghoul again. "The human world is too dangerous!" She shook her head. "Well, I'm in danger of losing my mind."

Realizing his daughter wasn't following him, Dracula had turned around to search for her. "Draculaura, where are you?" he called.

Draculaura lifted herself up. She turned into a bat again. She flew up, up, up, and as she did, she passed an old creepy-looking window with peeling paint. The light was on in an upstairs room. Her father saw her a moment later.

"What were you thinking?" he whispered. "Someone could have seen you."

What he didn't know was that someone *had* seen Draculaura. Peeking out of her bedroom window, Frankie Stein had marveled to watch a ghoul transform into a bat. Electricity flashed in her eyes.

Chapter 3

Fast Friends

If only Draculaura had someone to talk to other than her father and Webby. She just didn't know any other vampire ghouls. She paced back and forth in her room, frustrated. She flipped on her computer and began to record her vlog.

"I mean, I am almost sixteen hundred years old," she vented. "I'm extremely responsible. I do all my chores, I maintain every single cobweb in this house, and I'll always be stuck here, hiding in this attic, hidden from the world." She turned to address the webcam directly. "But at least I have you guys," she said cheerfully to her unseen viewers, "my trusty *Vampology* vlog followers."

She squinted to check out how many people were now subscribing to her posts. Zero. No one. She was sending her messages out into the world, and no one was listening and no one was watching. No one knew that there was a vampire teenager out there who needed a friend.

Except for her father.

Dracula had been coming up the stairs, and he heard his daughter talking to herself. He poked his head in through the door. "Oh…er…I was just…how about I make us a nice pot of bat tea?"

Draculaura tried to smile. Her father was so sweet. But he didn't understand how lonely she was. She wanted friends. Just as she was about to answer him, the doorbell rang.

The doorbell never rang.

Dracula looked at Draculaura. They were horrified. Who could it be?

Dracula raced out of the room and down the stairs, trying to be as quiet as possible. Draculaura followed him on tiptoe. Her father held his finger to his lips. They both listened. The bell rang again.

"Someone's at the door?" whispered Draculaura.

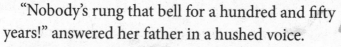

"Nobody's rung that bell for a hundred and fifty years!" answered her father in a hushed voice.

Someone was pounding on the door! "Hey, I know you're in there!"

Dracula looked at his daughter. "No one saw you, right?"

Draculaura gulped. She didn't think so. "Of course not. I was—"

"Hey! I know you're in there. I *saw* you! I saw you turn into a bat!"

Dracula glared at his daughter. What a disaster!

"Oops," whispered Draculaura. What was going to happen now that they were found out? Would they be driven out of town? Would they have to move?

The voice on the other side of the door called out again. "You can open up," it said. "I'm one of you."

What? Amazed, Draculaura tiptoed over to the door. She looked through the peephole.

Standing at the entranceway was a teenage ghoul. She had long black and white hair with silver highlights. She was wearing a totes adorable blue tank with a white collared shirt underneath.

Her skin was green. There were shiny bolts in her neck. There were stitches along her cheek and arm. As Draculaura watched, the ghoul casually pulled out the threads that attached her hand to her arm, held up her detached hand, and waved.

Draculaura gasped. This was *not* a normal ghoul! She swung the door open.

Dracula tried to stop her, but it was too late. The new ghoul had already stepped into the front hall.

"She's one of us!" Draculaura told her father. She'd never been so excited.

They told each other their names. They filled each other in on what it was like being a monster. All of this happened within the first five minutes of them meeting.

Draculaura led the new ghoul, Frankie Stein, into the living room. They had so much to tell each other about all the details of their lives. Dracula disappeared and returned with huge mugs of steaming bat tea.

"Thanks, Mr. D.," said Frankie. "It's really lovely of you to have me stay here."

Dracula's eyes widened. Draculaura rushed in

to explain. "She can share my bedroom."

"Whoa, whoa, whoa!" Dracula exclaimed. "Let's just pump the proverbial brakes for a minute here. I haven't seen another monster in decades. We still don't know who she is or where she came from."

"Like I said, I'm Frankie. My pops is Frankenstein. After the great monster Fright Flight, he went into hiding like all other monsters. Things get a bit boring when you're hiding out all by yourself."

"Tell me about it," agreed Draculaura.

Frankie tried to stifle a yawn. She was tired. It was almost morning.

"Come on," Draculaura urged her father. "You can't send her back. I never had a real friend before!"

"You have Webby," protested Dracula.

The spider, who had followed them downstairs on a thread, raised his head. "Huh?"

Draculaura batted sad puppy-dog eyes at her father. "Please?" she begged.

"That's not going to work on me." Her father crossed his arms under his cape. But he couldn't take his own eyes off his daughter's. He was transfixed. Hypnotized almost. Vampires could do that—glamour someone to obey them!

Draculaura's eyes grew wider. Her father's eyes grew wider. "I'm telling you, you are wasting your time…." he said softly.

Her father could not resist. He groaned, defeated. "Enough! Okay! She can stay!"

The ghouls hugged each other, delighted and relieved. They both had needed a friend for a long, long time. As tired as Frankie Stein was, she still wasn't ready to sleep. Draculaura took her up to the roof, and the girls spread out blankets and sleeping bags. A few last stars twinkled in the sky. The ghouls had so much still to learn about each other.

"Favorite color?" Draculaura asked Frankie.

"Electric blue! You?"

"Black," Draculaura answered instantly. "Definitely black. But also pink. Oh, oh, and sunlight!"

Frankie looked confused. "You're a vampire. Don't you burn in sunlight?"

"That's only in the movies." Draculaura laughed.

"Favorite song?"

Draculaura smiled "That's a no-brainer. 'Flawless.' It's Tash's new hit single."

"Who's Tash?" Frankie asked.

Draculaura couldn't believe it! "Who's Tash? Have you been hiding under a rock your whole life?"

"No, a secret lab, remember?" explained Frankie.

Without another word, Draculaura dashed down to her room and returned with armloads of posters, books, and magazines. Pictured on every one was the flawless, blond superstar.

"Tash is the world's most coolest, most awesome, amazing, beautiful rocker," enthused Draculaura. "I have all her albums, and I've seen all her videos, even the really super obscure one that she shot secretly in Tokyo."

"Oh, she's a Normie." Frankie was disappointed. "What's that?"

"Normie. Normal," explained Frankie. "A human."

Draculaura sighed, looking down at the photos of her idol. "Okay, big deal," she said at last. "Don't you think it's a bit unfair that humans are the only ones who get to be normal? I mean, who decided that turning into a bat and sleeping in a coffin was weird?"

"Tell me about it," Frankie agreed. "Just because I need a few stitches to stay together, that doesn't mean I'm not still a person."

Draculaura took a big breath. There was something she wanted to ask Frankie. "Do you ever wonder what it would be like, you know, to be normal?"

Frankie thought for a while. "I don't know. Being normal never really vibed with me. But it would be nice to do some normal things. Like have friends." She smiled at Draculaura.

"And throw parties." Draculaura grinned.

"And hang at a coffee shop and order elaborate-sounding drinks!"

"It could be a coffin shop!" Draculaura giggled. The girls were both daydreaming now.

"I love it," said Frankie. "And it could be right in the center of our little monster village, where monsters of all kinds could come to live together!"

"And go to school together!" Draculaura sighed wistfully.

"A real school!"

"We could call it…'Draculaura's Academy for Guys and Ghouls'! And Beasties. And…Others."

Frankie looked a little concerned.

"Yeah, no, bad idea," backtracked Draculaura.

"What about," suggested Frankie, "'School for the Scary, Strange, and Generally Unwelcome'!"

Draculaura smiled politely. Neither name was quite right. The name needed to be simple. It needed to be friendly. It needed to be inviting. Her face lit up. "Or we could just call it Monster High!"

"Monster High!" Frankie clapped her hands, delighted. The name was perfect. But then her face fell. It was just a name. It wasn't a real place. "If only we could. But it's impossible."

"Not impossible," said Draculaura, her voice determined. "Just challenging."

Draculaura remembered how earlier in the evening flying had seemed impossible. But she had figured it out. It just took a few tries. Draculaura could figure out this, especially since now she had a friend to help her.

Chapter 4

A Full-Moon Surprise

Frankie and Draculaura wanted to get started right away. There was no time to sleep. They knew they couldn't have a Monster High without students, and they were ready to hunt for their own monsters. They smiled at each other as they quietly sneaked out the front door. They could tell Draculaura's dad about their plans later.

The night was still dark, and all the human teenagers were home asleep, so they headed toward Normie Town. As they walked through the quiet streets, they listened. Except for the *chirp, chirp, chirp* of a few lone crickets, they heard nothing.

Draculaura peeked down a back alley. *"Hellooooo?"* she called in a low whisper. "Anybody out there?"

"Here, little monster-monsters," whispered Frankie.

"Ugh. This is hopeless," Draculaura realized.

"Wait!" Frankie held up her hand to Draculaura to quiet her. "Over there!" She pointed.

A trash can lid was clanking. A huge shadow loomed against the alley wall. Clutching each other's hands, the girls crept toward the dumpster. They peeked around it. Nibbling away on a leftover crust was a tiny mouse, its huge shadow behind it.

Draculaura was disappointed. "Forget it." She and Frankie felt defeated. They headed out of town. Only when they were far away from the alley did another creature emerge from behind the dumpster. It was a Mousicorn beastie with a horn coming out of her forehead! She squeaked. Like every other monster, she had learned how to hide.

Away from town the road ran through a desolate moor. Fog hung low. It was hard to see.

"Wait," suggested Frankie. "What about over there?"

"The moors? Nobody goes out there."
Draculaura shivered.

"Exactly!" exclaimed Frankie. "The perfect
hiding place for a monster."

The ghouls left the road, picking their way
around hillocks of grass and muddy puddles. The
fog grew thicker and thicker. Frankie let loose an
arc of electricity, illuminating their way.

Draculaura tried not to feel frightened. "Maybe
we should turn back."

"Hello? You're a vampire! You can't be afraid of
the dark."

Draculaura cleared her throat. "I'm not afraid
of the dark," she protested. But her voice quavered.
"Aaaaaaa!" she screamed a moment later.

A huge, hulking dark shadow had jumped in
front of them blocking their path.

"AAAAAAHHHHHHH!" screamed both
ghouls.

A shaft of moonlight broke through the dense
fog revealing the terrifying creature. It was an
enormous, squirming...pack of puppies!

They were jumping up and down. Their little
tongues where flopping out the sides of their
mouths. Their little black noses were wet. When

Frankie and Draculaura bent over to pet them, they were covered in puppy kisses.

"Hey!" Draculaura giggled. "Stop it! No! That tickles."

"Awwww," cooed Frankie. "There's a whole pack of little pups." She picked one up for a cuddle. "Aren't you just a wittle cutie pootie—"

"ROAR!"

A giant wolf was bearing down on the ghouls. Too late they realized that the puppies weren't just puppies. They were *wolf* pups, and this was their big sister. Her sharp teeth were bared. She growled menacingly.

Frankie and Draculaura each took a careful step backward. Their hearts were pounding in their chests.

"On the count of three…run!" Draculaura whispered to Frankie. "One, two—"

"Wait!" Frankie had noticed something. "Look at that amulet around the wolf's neck."

Sure enough, dangling through the sister wolf's fur was a moon pendant.

"Kind of strange for a wild wolf to be wearing an amulet," said Frankie. "Unless…"

"She's a monster!" realized Draculaura.

The wolf was still snarling at them. She looked very dangerous.

Frankie gulped. "I hope we are right." She took a step toward the wolf, who seemed surprised. "Excuse me," she began politely, "but you wouldn't happen to be a werewolf would you?"

The wolf growled menacingly.

Draculaura joined Frankie. "That's a shame. 'Cause we're looking for other monsters...like us."

The wolf stopped growling. She cocked her head. She understood what they were saying. Or it seemed like it anyway.

"We're forming a high school up on the hill. Monster High. It's where monsters go to be normal."

"Normal-ish," corrected Draculaura.

Frankie nodded her head. "Right. And we're even gonna have a coffin shop! With Mummy Mochas and everything."

The wolf's brown eyes widened, and a second later, she was transformed. Standing in front of Frankie and Draculaura was a slightly bedraggled but very pretty ghoul!

She had a thick mane of brown curly hair through which two tiny, furry ears poked delicately. She was dressed in a fierce green and purple outfit and didn't look anything like the wolf that she had been—except for two white gleaming fangs. She raised a single perfectly plucked eyebrow. Could she trust these ghouls?

"I would howl at the moon for a Mummy Mocha," she admitted. "Are you ghouls for real?"

Draculaura smiled. "We're getting the monsters back together. You in?"

The wolf puppies tumbled between the ghouls turning from humans back into pups and back again.

The weregirl, Clawdeen, looked down at her brothers protectively. "I've got a lot of brothers. And my mom."

"We have some extra room at my house," Draculaura offered.

Clawdeen thought for a moment. "This house? Does it have more than one overly crowded bathroom?"

"Well, yeah," answered Draculaura.

Clawdeen broke into huge grin. She was ready to move in with her whole family. And Monster High had another student.

Chapter 5

Every Vampire Needs a Pack of Puppies

Just after sunset, Dracula tiptoed into his daughter's room. He was carrying a tray with two steaming mugs of tea—one for Draculaura and one for Frankie. Right away, he noticed there was no one in the coffin. On the floor were a jumble of sleeping bags.

"Rise and dark!" Dracula announced.

Frankie stretched and yawned. Draculaura emerged from her sleeping bag with tousled hair. Clawdeen sat up, rubbing her eyes. "Hi!" she said.

"AHHHH!" screamed Dracula, totally startled. The tray in his hands tipped, spilling hot tea all over him. Draculaura grabbed a towel to dry him off.

"You okay, Dad?" she asked.

"Who is this?" he demanded. "Who is this stranger?"

Clawdeen put her hands on her hips, offended. "Who are you calling strange?"

"Dad!" Draculaura was mad at him for being so rude. "This is our *friend*, Clawdeen. She's a werewolf. We found her in the moors."

"And she really wants to live up here on the Hill," Frankie added.

Clawdeen nodded, running her hands through her tousled, wavy mane. "You have no idea what fifteen years of living in a den does to a ghoul's hair."

"Can she? Can she stay, Dad?" begged Draculaura.

Draculaura's eyes went wide and sad and hypnotic. She stared at her father. Frankie joined in, mesmerizing him with her expression.

"That might have worked once," Dracula

protested. "But I am not falling for it again."

Clawdeen stared at him with her saddest puppy-dog eyes. The three ghouls were giving it their all. Dracula bit his lip. He couldn't look away. He couldn't resist.

"It's not even that cute," he cried.

But it was. It was very cute. Especially when Clawdeen transformed into an actual wolf with round brown eyes and began to whimper. It was more than Dracula could bear.

"But this is the last one." He sighed.

The words were barely out of his mouth when the doorbell rang. He rushed down to answer it, and there was Clawdeen's mom with a stack of tiny suitcases beside her. Wolf pups tumbled into the front hall, jumping up on Dracula. They licked his face. They nibbled his ears. Puppies were everywhere.

What was he going to do? It was too late. He couldn't say no. Besides he really loved puppies.

Over the next few days as the Wolfs settled in, the puppies followed Dracula wherever he went. When he sat down, they got in his lap. When he got up, they chased after him. They licked his hands, his shoes, and his face. But Dracula always had a squeak toy ready to throw. One puppy would fetch and another would be waiting to play. They never got tired of playing!

Every day, Dracula was a little less grumpy than he'd been the day before.

He found some old picture books and began reading aloud to the puppies in front of the fire in the living room. Their favorite was *The Three Little Pigs*.

"And then he huffed and puffed and blew the house down. Not even the brick house could stop the Big Bad Wolf."

The Wolf puppies howled with delight.

Peeking in the living room, Draculaura smiled. "Pretty nice having other monsters around here, huh?"

Dracula glanced at Clawdeen's mom and blushed. He coughed. "You know, it really is."

The pups all cheered. One of them slathered a big sloppy kiss on Dracula's face.

Best of all, Dracula enjoyed having another grown-up monster around. In the early evenings, he and Clawdeen's mom would share a cup of bat tea and look at old family photo albums together. Draculaura had never seen her father so happy. And she had never been so happy. But there was something she wanted even more than a big family. She was still dreaming about Monster High.

Chapter 6

Calling All Monsters

Draculaura and Frankie were determined to turn the old, run-down mansion into a first-rate school—and that was going to take a lot of work. All the ghouls and the puppies hammered and sawed and sandpapered and painted over the next few weeks. Walking down the halls, peeking into rooms that would become dormitories and classrooms, Draculaura was pleased. "The place isn't looking half bad, if I do say so myself."

The enormous banquet hall had been turned into a Creepateria with long tables at which the future students would eat. Frankie decorated each table with floating green candles. They looked creeptastic.

There was only one thing missing: monsters.

Draculaura was still working on her *Vampology* vlog, and she still had no subscribers. She was recording herself in her bedroom while Clawdeen flipped through a fashion magazine. She was on the hunt for the perfect hairstyle, and she hadn't found it yet.

Draculaura stared into the camera on her computer. "And we're determined to rescue the monsters of the world. The freaky, the beastly, and the downright weird! Only how do we find you?"

She sighed as she shut off the webcam. She refreshed her vlog page. No one had watched her message. "Isn't anybody listening?"

Frankie looked up from a

chemistry book she'd been studying. "Well, you're not gonna reach monsters like that. No wonder your vlog doesn't have any listeners. You're using normal Internet."

"Uh, yeah," said Draculaura. "That's how it's done."

"Uh, yeah," repeated Clawdeen. "If you're normal."

Frankie sighed. "You gotta use the Monster Web." She reached past Draculaura and began typing furiously on the keyboard.

"There's a Monster Web?" Draculaura had no idea!

The computer's screen went blank for a second. Frankie pushed on two keys simultaneously, and a new hot-pink-and-black screen appeared. Frankie dragged Draculaura's vlog over to the new Monster window. Frankie shook her head. "You haven't even been broadcasting all this time." She continued typing.

The graphics on the screen changed again. "Behold the Monster Web. Available anytime, anywhere." Frankie stepped back so Draculaura could get a good look at it.

"Mind blown," said Draculaura. Excited, she refreshed her web page.

Nothing happened. Oh well. At least they'd tried.

Frankie was tired and already getting into her sleeping bag. Webby swung across the room and switched off the light. It was time for the ghouls to go to bed. Draculaura crawled into her coffin.

As the ghouls slept, monsters all over the world were making a surprising discovery. A very surprising discovery. And far, far away, a glamorous zombie smiled to herself. A monster high school? Oh, this was very interesting, very interesting indeed. Her smile turned into a wicked grin.

Chapter 7

Freaky Field Trip

Draculaura screamed.

Her ear-piercing cry caused her father to jump up and flip his breakfast plate into the air and over onto the floor.

Frankie and Clawdeen woke up and saw Draculaura staring at her computer screen. She was shaking her head; she was laughing; she was screaming. The ghouls clustered close. *They* screamed!

Dracula raced up upstairs to Draculaura's room. What was the matter? What was going on? What had happened?

"What is it? What is it?" he demanded to know as he stormed into the room.

"What is what?" asked Clawdeen.

"Whatever it is that you are screaming about?"

Draculaura turned to her father. She was beaming. "Monster High has students!" She was so excited that she was talking a mile a minute. "I put out a call on my *Vampology* vlog. Frankie taught me how to post it on the Monster Web. She's a tech genius."

Frankie shrugged. "It's kinda my thing."

"Anyway," continued Draculaura, "we got, like, a zillion e-mails this morning! And, Dad...Dad?"

She noticed that he had a bit of toast stuck to his head. "You've got a little something...." She picked it off gently.

Clawdeen was jumping up and down she was so happy. "The monsters are coming! The monsters are coming!" She stopped, realizing something for the first time. "Wait! How are they getting here?"

Frankie turned to Draculaura. "You can fly, right?"

Draculaura nodded. What did Frankie mean?

"Maybe if I just use my electricity to supercharge you…before you take off," Frankie suggested. She rubbed her hands together, and an arc of pure electricity sizzled between them when she pulled them apart.

"Whoa, whoa, whoa!" Draculaura jumped backward. "Put it in reverse. Nobody's electrocuting anybody."

Throughout all of this, Dracula was watching the ghouls, thinking. At last, he spoke. "If you're going to collect these monsters, you're going to do it the old-fashioned way."

"I love the old-fashioned way," exclaimed Frankie.

"And you are going to wear helmets," Dracula warned.

Clawdeen touched her hair. "Helmets? You got any idea what that does to all this hair?"

Dracula gave her a stern look. "Do you want to reach the other monsters or not?"

It was a matter of minutes before Clawdeen had a helmet on and so did Frankie and Draculaura.

Dracula led the ghouls down to the library. He turned himself into a bat and flew up to the highest bookshelf where he grabbed hold of an old wooden box with his feet. What was he up to? Where were they going? And how?

When he was back at floor level, he transformed into himself. He slid open the box. "Haven't used this thing in centuries. Hope it still works."

Frankie peered at it. "What exactly is it?"

Whatever was inside of the box was glowing a warm, hazy pink.

"This," explained Dracula, "is a Monster Mapalogue." He unfolded the sides of the box to reveal an engraved wooded board. Attached to it with a silver chain was a small skull.

"Cool!" Clawdeen was impressed.

"Wow," whispered Draculaura, awed.

"That's clever," agreed Frankie.

Dracula beckoned them to come closer. "In ages past, monsters used the Mapalogue to locate one another. But when the humans turned against us during the great Fright Flight, our kind all went into hiding for our protection. After that, there really didn't seem to be a use for this thing anymore."

"Until now!" Draculaura gasped.

Frankie's brow was furrowed. "So how does it work?"

"First, you place your fingers gently on the Skullette," Dracula instructed.

Very carefully, the ghouls touched their fingertips to the tiny skull.

"Now," continued Dracula, "you say the name of the monster you're trying to reach."

Draculaura pulled out her iCoffin and scrolled to her e-mail. She looked at the first monster who had contacted her. "First up…Cleo. But she says she's a bit tied up. What now?"

Dracula looked from Frankie to Clawdeen to Draculaura. "Are you sure you want to do this?"

"Totes!"

"Yes!"

"Obviously," said Clawdeen.

Dracula took a deep breath. "Okay. Say the magic words. *Exsto monstrum.* So all together…"

"Cleo! Exsto monstrum!"

Nothing happened.

Frankie picked up the skull. She shook it. "This thing doesn't even work." She was about to turn it over to see if there was a switch when…*Poof!*

The ghouls vanished from the library.

They opened their eyes and blinked. The ghouls were hovering in the air above a vast stretch of desert! They gasped and flopped into the sand, spluttering.

"Oof!"

"Owww!"

Clawdeen touched her helmet. "Guess these things come in handy after all!"

"The Mapalogue worked!" exclaimed Frankie. "Where are we?"

"Ghouls!" Draculaura pointed behind them. They were standing right in front of an enormous Egyptian pyramid.

Draculaura grinned. Right in front of them was a door.

Chapter 8

A Royal Recruit

Inside, the pyramid was dark and musty. The walls were covered in ancient hieroglyphics.

Draculaura loved it. "Fangtastic!" she exclaimed as the ghouls walked down the narrow passageway.

All around them were doors leading to the undiscovered tombs of mummies.

Which one led to Cleo?

"We're going to have to explore all these tombs," Frankie realized.

Draculaura casually pushed on one door to open it. Screams and moans echoed from inside.

Light blasted out of the darkness and singed Draculaura's hair. She slammed the door shut.

Her face white, she shuddered. "It's not that one."

Clawdeen's wolf ears twitched. She was listening to something. She walked over to the entranceway of another tomb. It was encrusted with glowing jewels. From far away the ghouls could hear soft angelic voices singing. "I've got a feelin' it might be this one," whispered Clawdeen.

The ghouls nodded to one another. They approached the door. A ray of sunlight from far above them had found its way through a crack. It lit up a jeweled scarab. Inside of the scarab was a handprint. Should the ghouls place their hands on the handprint? Was it safe?

Draculaura knew what she had to do. She touched the scarab. It pulsed with light. Gears clanked somewhere in the pyramid. Smoke billowed all around them so that they could barely see. The door slid open. Stone steps led up, up, up.

Standing on the topmost step, a pile of bandages at her feet, was a very trendy young Egyptian princess.

Her dark-brown hair was streaked with gold. She had bandages wrapped around her arms and legs. She was wearing lots of gold jewelry.

She clapped her hands, delighted. "You're here!"

She skipped elegantly down the steps and hugged each of the ghouls dramatically.

"You must be Cleo," said Draculaura a little shyly.

"The one and only Cleo de Nile." The mummy princess smiled.

"I'm Draculaura, this is Frankie, and that over there is Clawdeen," Draculaura explained. "We're

your Monster High student outreach committee. Anything we can help with, just ask!"

"Oh fabulous!" exclaimed Cleo. "It's been a *millennium* since I had help. My luggage is over there. Do be careful carrying them. Those jewels are on loan from the pharaoh."

The ghouls looked up the stairs and saw trunk after heavy trunk overflowing with jewels and gems.

Frankie cleared her throat. "I'm afraid there won't be room for those at the Monster High dorms. But don't worry, we've got all the basics."

Cleo let out a sigh of relief. "A personal chef?"

"There's a great Creepateria," Draculaura explained apologetically.

"A royal masseuse?" asked Cleo.

The ghouls shook their heads.

Cleo was trying not to appear alarmed. "Ruby-encrusted lounging throne?"

The ghouls looked down at their feet, clearly embarrassed. But Cleo surprised them. "At least I finally have friends," she said.

"That's right!" said Frankie, breathing a sigh of relief.

And with that, the ghouls made their way back to Draculaura's house.

No one got any sleep that night! The ghouls were up late giggling and laughing and getting to know one another. None of them had ever been to a slumber party before. There were secrets to share. There were snacks to eat. They all had their first pillow fight!

"Hey, Drac, you forgot your pillow!" said Clawdeen, and whomped her in the face.

"What's going on up there?" shouted Dracula from downstairs. "Go to sleep!"

The ghouls turned off the light, but it was a long time before they stopped giggling.

Cleo was the last to fall asleep. She might not have her jewels or her luggage or her throne, but this was a lot better than being all alone in a sandy old pyramid. Thank goodness for Monster High.

Chapter 9

Creature Feature

Now that the ghouls had the Mapalogue, finding other monsters was a snap. After painting one another's nails, the ghouls were ready to go the next night. They put on their helmets. They placed their fancy fingertips on the Skullette.

"*Lagoona! Exsto monstrum!*" they announced together.

Poof!

"*Ow!*"

"*Oh!*"

"*Oof*"

Wherever they were, it was wet. A wave broke

over their heads. Cleo spit out a mouthful of seaweed. Clawdeen shook the water out of her hair. Frankie brushed the sand off her hands. Draculaura looked up and saw a sporty ghoul on a surfboard headed right toward them.

Her blond hair, streaked with the color of sea foam, wafted behind her. She leaped into the air as the wave curled, flipped off her board, and landed lightly on the beach. Her board hurled toward shore and drove into the sand.

"Oy, mates!" she said to the ghouls. She had an Australian accent!

"Lagoona Blue!" Draculaura guessed it must be her.

"Nice to meet you!"

"We're from Monster High."

"Awesome skills," complemented Frankie.

"G'day, roomie," said Lagoona to Cleo. Cleo laughed nervously. She'd never had a roommate before.

Lagoona whipped out a phone shaped like a clamshell and snapped a photo. Cleo smiled for the camera. Whatever differences she might have with these ghouls, they were all monsters. They were better off together than they were alone.

Soon there were enough students to have classes at Monster High—and the first teacher was Draculaura's dad. On the first day of class, everyone was nervous. Especially Draculaura.

"Dad's late," she worried.

"Can't wait to start learning stuff!" barked one of the pups.

"So what's this first class about?" Clawdeen wondered.

Frankie looked into her book bag. "I think I brought enough school supplies."

Cleo sniffed, staring at the Wolf pups. "I didn't know they allowed pets in the classroom."

When they weren't in class, the ghouls were hunting for more students. They headed to a tropical swamp filled with man-eating flowers, three-eyed frogs, and other beasties. Inside of a beautiful, thorny blossom was a tiny, very sleepy swamp monster—Marshall. His hair was colorful and thorny.

He was adorable, and all the ghouls wanted to pet him. Except for Frankie, who was almost swallowed whole by a giant Venus flytrap.

Luckily, the ghouls rescued her just in time and whisked her back to Monster High with Marshall. Recruiting students could be dangerous!

On another trip, they headed over to Greece. In addition to their helmets, they wore protective goggles. This monster turned anyone who met his eyes into stone! He was a mythic gorgon. His hair was made out of hissing snakes. When they discovered him, he was standing in a garden surrounded by the sculptures of soldiers, their swords raised. When the ghouls handed him a pair of cool shades, the soldiers came back to life—and charged the ghouls and Deuce Gorgon. Again, they got away just in time. Monster High had another student!

Deuce Gorgon high-fived Marshall when he arrived in class.

A few days later, the ghouls found themselves in another back alley looking into another dumpster. Inside of this one was a round, bloated goblin named Gob. Spit dribbled from his mouth as he tossed day-old donuts and slimy wrappers into his mouth. His breath was bad, his face was greasy, but he was a monster and that was that.

The moment Gob saw Cleo, he leaped into her arms. She tried to hide her disgust as he slobbered on a mold-covered cookie. The other ghouls tried to hide their laughter. *Phew!* Was she ever relieved when they left him to get settled in his dorm room!

The ghouls' next trip was to the Arctic. Trapped in a giant block of ice was a prehistoric mammoth beastie standing next to an ice sprite. They were both holding their iCoffins. What had frozen them in the midst of reaching out to Draculaura?

Luckily, Clawdeen had a hair dryer and Frankie superpowered it with a jolt of electricity. The ice was melted in no time. Woolee hugged Draculaura. Crystal hugged Cleo—and Cleo was instantly encased in her own ice block. Uh-oh! Crystal had to learn how to use her magic if she was going to come to Monster High.

Not all the students came to Monster High with the help of the Mapalogue. As word spread, some monsters had themselves mailed to the new school. One box full of bones arrived with an instruction manual.

Draculaura scratched her head as she looked at the complicated diagrams. With the help of the other ghouls, she began assembling two skeletons. When their skulls were attached, Skelly and his brother, Bonesy, rattled their bones happily.

The monsters loved the Coffin Kiosk and hung out after their class, catching up. Gob's favorite was the Green Coffin Shake. Woolee often let Crystal sit on her tusk while they both slurped mocha lattes. Lagoona made a sign for the hangout, and Frankie electrified it so it flashed and sparkled invitingly.

Dracula's classes were now so full they were in the auditorium. There was only one empty seat left, and it was Gob's. The goblin with the jelly belly squeezed down the row and plopped into it happily.

Clawdeen's mom was teaching art. Her art studio was decorated with picture of all the monsters' families—the vampires, the werewolves, the yetis, the swamp things, and all different kinds of beasties.

"Art is your soul flowing onto the canvas," explained Mrs. Wolf, walking around the room as the students worked at their easels. The model in the front of the class struck a pose. It was Skelly!

"Try to capture the essence of Skelly." She looked at Cleo's drawing. "I like where that is going." She smiled at Frankie's. "Oh, that's nice!" She removed a drawing from Gob's mouth. "Don't eat the paper," she warned him.

When she got to Clawdeen's work, Mrs. Wolf shook her head. Her daughter had drawn Skelly, pretty much perfectly, but over him she had added an absolutely fabulous outfit.

"Clawdeen!" reprimanded her mother. "This is not fashion camp. This is art class!"

Clawdeen rolled her eyes. "Fashion *is* art, Mom."

A latecomer peeked into the studio. He was tall and handsome and wraith-thin. He had a shock of silver-white hair. He glanced at Clawdeen's drawing admiringly. "I for one think your design is sick."

"I don't remember asking for your opinion, Rayth," answered Clawdeen defensively.

"I am sure he means that as a compliment!" Draculaura whispered to her friend.

Clawdeen blushed. "Oh! Well, I guess it is sick!"

The bell rang.

"Remember, tomorrow we have a very special guest model! Invisible Dan!" Mrs. Wolf announced happily.

"How are we supposed to draw him if he's invisible?" Cleo wondered.

Out in the hall, monsters were putting away their books in their coffin-shaped lockers before lunch. Woolee towered over all the other students. Crystal took a sip at the drinking fountain—and froze it.

A giant beastie with tons of tentacles managed the Creepateria—serving food, ringing up the register, collecting trays, cleaning up spills.

"So what's on the menu today?" Clawdeen asked as she got into line.

"Mash," said the lunch lady. "Everybody gets the mash."

Clawdeen's nose wrinkled as the lady plopped a gray spoonful onto her tray.

"Is the lunch lady okay?" Frankie wondered.

"The food's not," whispered Clawdeen.

Lagoona used her tray as a surfboard and skidded down the banister to her table. The lunch lady gave her a thumbs-up from one of her tentacles. The Wolf pups cheered.

Frankie put her tray away and went over to the dessert case. All that was left were crumbs. "Where's all the dessert?" she asked the lunch lady.

A tentacle pointed across the Creepateria to Gob. He was covered in icing and crumbs. He reached into his own bloated belly, pulled out a gnawed-on donut, and gobbled it up again. Yuck!

"I did not need to see that." Clawdeen shuddered.

"Keep away!" agreed another monster.

Draculaura looked around the chaotic scene. The food needed to be better. They needed more teachers. They needed a few rules at least. "This school is getting crazy," she said.

"How about a student body council?" Frankie suggested. "Draculaura for student body president!"

Draculaura's eyes brightened. "How about we all run together? As a team?

Lagoona shook her head. "Oh, I wish I could, but I already volunteered to be captain of the new swim team. And we need all the help we can get."

Lagoona thought about the team's first practice at the pool. Gob showed up wearing water wings. He cannonballed from the diving board—and all the water in the pool sloshed out.

Draculaura turned to Cleo. "What about you?"

"Thanks, but I'm already royalty," she answered. "And besides, I've got my hands full trying to get my grade up in science class."

She tried not to think about her chemistry catastrophe earlier in the day. Frankie's tubes and flasks were all filled with a swirling purple liquid while Cleo's overflowed with molten gold. Even worse, the gold exploded!

Clawdeen was too busy to help out as well. "You know I would help you, but I'm just getting into my groove at the gardening club."

It wasn't the planting that Clawdeen enjoyed as much as the pruning. She loved turning ordinary bushes into high-fashion designs. And she was really good at it—as long as Rayth didn't startle her and make her give one of her topiary trees a buzz cut.

Still, Draculaura was sure she'd find the right ghoul for the job, and there was only one more to ask—Frankie.

She smiled at Draculaura. "Look no further, ghoulfriend. I'll run for student council with you!"

"You will?"

"Sure," said Frankie. "I've got a lot of time on my hands now."

Frankie reached out to shake Draculaura's hand—and shocked her.

But Draculaura just laughed. "Put it there, partner."

Together, she and Frankie had found students for Monster High. Now they had to organize those students so Monster High could be the best school ever. How hard could that be?

Chapter 10

A Creeperific Campaign

Draculaura was back on her vlog to get the word out. Frankie was sitting beside her. The other ghouls were offering support and waving flags and cheering for their ghoulfriends.

"That's right," announced Frankie, "we're running for Monster High's very first president."

"Copresidents," explained Draculaura. "And a vote for Frankie and Drac is a vote for monsters everywhere!"

Frankie nodded in agreement. "We bring to you our vision of a world in which monsters can finally live peacefully side by side with the human world. I know you're skeptical, but it *can* happen. And with our dedication and determination, it will!"

"And we promise to celebrate with our first-ever school dance, planned by Miss Cleo de Nile herself. Dancing the Fright Away!" Draculaura smiled at the camera.

"So remember," added Frankie. "Vote for Frankie and Drac, 'cause these monsters got yo' back."

"Plus, we're the only ones running." Draculaura shrugged apologetically as she turned off the webcam.

"I think that went well," decided Frankie.

The other ghouls agreed. What could possibly go wrong?

Frankie and Draculaura were enjoying their campaign. They passed out chocolate pops in

the shape of their faces to the students lounging outside the Creepateria.

"Vote for Drac and Frankie!" announced Frankie. "Help monsters come out of the dark!"

"Vote for Frankie and Draculaura!" exclaimed Draculaura. "And we'll have megastar Tash come to our school dance!"

Frankie looked at her friend, stunned. Where did this promise come from? How could they possibly get Tash to Monster High?

Draculaura blushed. "Too much?" she realized. But it was too late. All the students had heard her promise, and they were excited.

"Really?"

"Wow!"

"Tash!"

Word was spreading like wildfire.

The loudspeaker crackled. "Will Frankie Stein and Draculaura please report to the headmaster's office? Immediately," boomed Dracula's voice.

Oh no. They were in trouble.

Draculaura swallowed hard. "Maybe a little much."

Her father was pacing back and forth angrily

when they arrived in his office. Draculaura and Frankie quietly settled into their chairs.

Dracula whirled around. "Megastar Tash is coming to your dance?"

Draculaura looked at her father with her soulful eyes. "It doesn't hurt to promise."

Dracula grumbled to himself as he paced.

"This is politics, Professor D.," chimed in Frankie.

Dracula held up a poster for Dancing the Fright Away. At its center was a sparkling photo of Tash, surrounded by disco balls. "You put her face on the poster!"

Frankie tried to explain. "Cleo says it's impossible to say no to royalty."

"Plus, I think if Tash got to know us, she might like us and come." It hadn't been an empty promise for Draculaura; she really wanted to invite her idol to perform.

"I think we're very likable," added Frankie.

Dracula was furious. "This is a *secret* monster high school," he bellowed.

"It's just a dance!" protested Draculaura.

The intercom buzzed. "Mr. Headmaster, sir.

We've got a situation with the snack machine."

Dracula pushed the button to respond. "Can't it wait?"

"I think you'll want to see this," answered the secretary's voice.

Draculaura and Frankie followed Dracula to the Creepateria. A hub of students was clustered around the snack machine. Gob was stuck inside of it.

"How could he even fit?" Dracula wondered.

Gob was stuffing candy bars and potato chips and wrappers into his mouth.

"Everybody, I insist on calm," Dracula ordered. "Gob, extract your person from that dispenser immediately."

Dracula reached his arm up into the machine and tried to pull out Gob with a tug. But after devouring so many snack foods, he was too bloated to squeeze out via the slot he'd got in through. He was stuck.

Dracula found a key to open up the whole front of the machine. What a catastrophe!

"He didn't say no to the dance," Draculaura whispered to Frankie.

"Which is sort of another way of saying yes!" Frankie said hopefully.

Clawdeen was hurrying down the hall. She had an urgent message for Draculaura. "Ghouls! We have a report of a monster off the grid."

"This ghoul hasn't spoken to another monster in years," explained Cleo. "Her name's Moanica."

"Poor Moanica!" sighed Draculaura. "Think how excited she'll be when we show up."

It was time to get the Mapalogue and bring another student to Monster High.

Chapter 11

Zombie Alert!

Tombstones and marble crypts stretched as far as the eye could see. An eerie layer of fog blanketed the cemetery. The ghouls landed on a heap near a creepy mausoleum.

"*Ooh!*"

"*Ow!*"

"*Ouch!*"

Traveling never got easier. Clawdeen took off her helmet and shook out her hair. "You sure we're in the right place?" she wondered.

Somewhere, a door creaked on rusty hinges.

"Supposedly," said Cleo.

Clawdeen shivered. "And I thought living in a den was bad."

A moan broke the silence followed by another and another. The moaning sounds were coming closer. Emerging from behind the tombstones and from within the crypts were...zombies!

"Whoa!" screamed Clawdeen.

Leading the pack of mindless followers was a gorgeously creepy teenage zombie girl.

"Hey, hey, hey," muttered the zombies. The Zomboyz were wearing pressed khakis and brightly colored sweaters of prep-school students. But their eyes were blank black pools. They did whatever the girl told them to. That was clear.

"Who dares trespass my cemetery?" she demanded to know.

"Your cemetery?" Clawdeen couldn't imagine wanting to stay in such a miserable place, much less rule over it.

Draculaura stepped forward, smiling. "Moanica. Moanica D'Kay, right?"

She bared her teeth. "Who's asking?" She extended her long-taloned fingers.

"Whoa, whoa." Draculaura stepped backward.

"There's no need to get scratchy. I'm Draculaura.
And this is Cleo, Clawdeen, Frankie, and
Lagoona. We're just like you." She gave the zombie
girl a friendly smile.

"Wrong!" shouted Moanica.

"She's telling the truth," explained Frankie
nervously. "We're monsters. See?" She twisted
off her arm and held it out to Moanica. "Wanna
shake on it?"

"I don't do handshakes," answered Moanica
haughtily. "But I could use a few
more monsters in my Zomboyz
Army." She cackled. "We've
already taken this cemetery back
from the humans. Next we'll
conquer the entire human world!"

Lightning flashed. Frankie
applauded. "Sounds ambitious!
Speaking of ambition,
why don't you come
back to our school?"

"School?" Moanica
snorted. "You don't get it.
I'm not going anywhere.

And neither are you. Zomboyz!" She snapped her fingers, and the zombies began staggering toward the ghouls.

The ghouls formed a close circle protectively.

"Listen, Zomboyz, we have room for you too," Frankie suggested.

"Yes, everyone is welcome at Monster High." Draculaura tried to sound as friendly and inviting as she could under the circumstances. "Why don't we all just take a deep breath and talk this out?"

The Zomboyz didn't seem to be listening. They were getting closer and closer.

Clawdeen was worried. "Ghoul, look at them. I don't think they talk...or breathe."

The Zomboyz lunged forward awkwardly, but Lagoona charged through them. They scattered, confused. Lagoona leaped to the top of a mausoleum. "*Oooh*, little Zomboyz," she called. "Catch me if you can!"

The ghouls exchanged glances. It was worth a try.

Lagoona was leaping from tombstone to mausoleum to tombstone. The Zomboyz were confused. One of them reached out for Cleo's

Draculaura and Frankie Stein search for monsters to bring to Monster High!

Lagoona Blue, fintastic surfer ghoul, can't wait to go to Monster High!

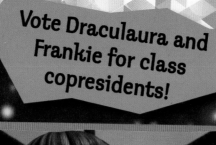

Vote Draculaura and Frankie for class copresidents!

Moanica campaigns to help monsters come out of the dark.

Frankie, Lagoona, Clawdeen, Cleo, and Draculaura...creeperific friends forever!

The ghouls are all dressed up and ready to dance the fright away!

Ari Hauntington is right at home at Monster High!

WELCOME TO
MONSTER HIGH

Monster High
is here to stay!

neck. In a flash, she wrapped him up from head to toe in some of the extra mummy bandages she always carried. Mummified, he toppled over. Cleo yawned, bored. She'd seen worse in the pyramids.

Clawdeen clambered to the top of a crypt. She looked up at the sky, hoping that the fog would clear, if just for a second. "Come on, moonlight, don't fail me now."

It didn't. A wild howl ripped through the cemetery. Clawdeen was a werewolf. The Zomboy who had been chasing her turned away, frightened, and went after Cleo. But Clawdeen leaped onto his back and pinned him down with her paws.

Draculaura transformed into a bat. She flapped her wings in the face of another Zomboy and emitted a piercing high-pitched ultrasonic screech. The Zomboy covered his ears and sank to the ground.

But flying was still hard for Draculaura. She zigged and zagged through the air, and a whole legion of Zomboyz started chasing her. Seeing that she was in trouble, Cleo stretched linen between two headstones. Boom! Boom! Boom!

Every one of the Zomboyz tripped over it and tumbled downhill.

Meanwhile, Frankie was keeping the Zomboyz at arm's length, literally. She had detached her arm and was using it as a sword. When she tripped into a patch of mud, she was electrified with anger. The bolts on her neck sparked. "That's it, boys," she shouted. "I'm done playing nice!" Frankie reattached her arm, clenched her fist, and zapped a Zomboy with a jolt of electricity.

Lagoona was on her surfboard, whizzing across the tops of the tombstones like they were the crests of waves. The Zomboyz were in hot pursuit. On a curved railing, she whipped around unexpectedly and sped forward toward them. She knocked them all off into an open tomb. She slammed shut the door and bolted it shut. *Phew!*

The rest of the Zomboyz had been defeated by the ghouls as well. They were spread out across the cemetery, rubbing their heads and groaning.

Clawdeen and Draculaura had transformed back into ghouls again.

Clawdeen dusted off her skirt. "Where's Moanica? I'd like to finish our conversation."

"She's not worth it," said Lagoona, still catching her breath.

Draculaura was sad that they couldn't help Moanica. "I wish she had listened...."

They had defeated the Zomboyz, but they had not found another student for Monster High. Disappointed, they put their hands on the Skullette and disappeared.

But Moanica had been watching them from behind a gravestone. Her eyes narrowed. It was one thing to rule over a cemetery—it was another altogether to take over an entire high school.

Where should she begin?

Chapter 12

A Monster with Pride

Classes were in full swing back at Monster High. Chalk squeaked, students drummed their claws and flippers, the bell rang. Lockers opened and shut as students rushed to exchange their pencils and books.

When Clawdeen headed to her next class, Rayth waved at her. A lock of his silver-white hair fell across his forehead. Clawdeen blushed.

Dracula was getting ready to lecture in the front of the room. In front of him was an odd assortment of normal human things—things monsters never used. Pizza. Eyeglasses. Money.

Dracula held up a dollar bill. "Can anyone tell me what this might be used for in the human world?

Venus McFlytrap raised her hand. "*Ooooh, ooooh, oooh!* I know! It's one of those thingies humans hold to their nose when it leaks!"

Dracula shook his head, sighing. "That's a tissue. Anyone else?"

No one raised their hand.

In the bathroom, Clawdeen was adjusting her jacket. She was earning a reputation as Monster High's fashionista—and even Woolee was seeking her out for hair-styling advice.

Wherever Clawdeen went, Rayth seemed to be just around the corner. Every time she walked past, he got all flustered.

"Looking good," he told her when she came out of the bathroom. But he was so distracted, he walked into an open locker door.

Outside the Creepateria, Cleo was working on posters for Dancing the Fright Away. Deuce Gorgon was helping her decorate. He always made sure to wear his shades these days—so he wouldn't turn his friends to stone. He was standing on a ladder hanging heavy lights. Cleo was directing him and also talking on her iCoffin. "Yes. I'm looking to book Tash. It's an exclusive event."

"Uh, Cleo?" Deuce called. He was tottering on the ladder.

"A little to the left," instructed Cleo, without looking. "What do you mean it's not important enough? Don't you know who I am?" Her face was red with fury, and she was yelling into the phone. "Tell your client that she's the one missing out!"

Cleo angrily hung up the phone. She looked up at Deuce. "Perfect," she said.

Just at that moment, Deuce lost his grip, tumbling off the ladder. The lamps fell on his head. "Whoa! *Ow!*"

Posters for Frankie and Draculaura were everywhere. They were ready to be Monster High's very first copresidents. After all, no one else was running against them.

They gathered at the coffin shop for bubbling bat tea and green smoothies.

"I'm telling you, you two are shoo-ins for student council," said Clawdeen.

"You think?" worried Draculaura. "What if someone else decides to run against us?"

"You're the school's founders." Lagoona laughed. "Who would run against you?"

Little did they know, that Moanica D'Kay and her Zomboyz were headed to Monster High.

"Time to put on your happy face, Zomboyz," she instructed them. "You're students now."

In perfect unison, the Zomboyz smiled. They all had rotten teeth.

Ghouls clustered around the bar at the coffin shop. They were talking about the upcoming election and the first dance.

"I'm so excited!"

"When is the election again? I can't wait!"

"What's the first thing you want to do as copresident?" Draculaura asked Frankie.

"Maybe start a monster science committee!"

A passing monster looked down at the mash on his plate. "Do you think the food's any better?"

"It's possibly even worse than yesterday," answered his friend.

Overhearing them, Frankie made a mental note to review the meals when she was copresident.

A loud cackle caught everyone's attention. The monsters at the Coffin Kiosk stopped talking.

"Well, isn't this just peachy!" It was Moanica D'Kay. "I'm sorry, was I interrupting?" She smiled wickedly.

Draculaura whirled around. "Moanica! What are you doing here?"

Moanica pretended to be hurt, clutching her heart. She sauntered around the Coffin Kiosk as if she already owned the monster coffee lounge. She ran a finger along a table, checking for dust. She picked up a monster's cup, took a sip, and threw it on the floor in disgust. She ambled over to Gob, who threw his hands over his milk shake. Moanica poked his gooey belly and pulled away a slimy finger. She wiped it on Deuce's shirt.

"Draculaura." She sighed dramatically. "Frankly, I'm a little hurt. You invited me to this school after all. Everyone is welcome. Isn't that what you said?"

"She's got a point." Frankie winced.

"Besides," continued Moanica, "I had to

see this place for myself. So many, many monsters to recruit..." She cleared her throat and corrected herself. "I mean, befriend."

Cleo walked over to her. "Sorry, Moanica. You'll have to grow your Zomboyz Army somewhere else. Monster High is a peaceful place."

"Peaceful?" Moanica laughed. "Isn't that adorable, Zomboyz?"

But her obedient army wasn't paying attention! They were ordering coffee, relaxing in the easy chairs, sipping smoothies.

"Zomboyz!" Monica yelled.

Draculaura seized the opportunity to convince them all to come to Monster High. "Our school teaches monsters how to come out of the dark," she said.

"Just one little problem," Monica sneered. "You're still in hiding." She jumped up on a table. "If you really want to come out of the dark," she addressed the guys and ghouls, "you've gotta remind humans we exist."

Her words caused a stir.

"We will. When they're ready," protested Frankie.

"Go home, Moanica," Clawdeen ordered. "No one wants to hear your nasty plans."

But Moanica wasn't listening. She was studying Frankie and Draculaura's election posters. She grabbed one off the nearest wall. "I think we should let the students decide what they want to hear." She snapped her fingers.

In an instant, the Zomboyz had created election posters—with Moanica's face in profile.

"That's right, students of Monster High. You now have a choice for who you want to lead this school's student council. You can vote Frankie and Drac, the monsters who hide. Or Moanica D'Kay, the monster with *pride*!"

She leaped off the table and strutted past Draculaura and Frankie. "See you on the ballot, ghouls."

What were Frankie and Draculaura going to do? This was a whole new campaign.

Chapter 13

Scare Tactics

Frankie was working on an experiment in chemistry class. Beakers bubbled, steam rose, sparks shot across the room. Frankie ignited a burner with a jolt from her fingertip.

Lagoona was trying to pay attention. But she was worried. "Moanica can't win the election, right?" she whispered to Cleo.

"She won't," Cleo answered confidently. She went to pour a pink powder into one of Frankie's test tubes, but Frankie swatted her hand away.

"But what if she does?" asked Frankie.

"Ghoul, please." Clawdeen laughed. She was

braiding a strand of her hair. "No one's going to
vote for Moanica. That zombie's a menace."

A three-eyed frog in the corner blinked in
agreement.

But Frankie wasn't so sure. "I've seen more
than one monster in here wearing a MOANICA FOR
PRESIDENT pin. What does she have that we don't?"
She glanced across the room, where Moanica was
talking to another group of ghouls.

"Well, for one…pins," said Cleo. "But two, she's
got a message." She held up one of the pins that
Moanica had given her.

Lagoona read the words on it out loud: *"Why
hide? Vote for Monsters with Pride. Moanica
D'Kay for President."*

"We're not hiding!" Draculaura protested.
"We're all here together, aren't we? We're just
preparing…in secret. On a hill. Where no one can
see us." She thought about what she'd just said.
"Ghouls? What if Moanica is right? What if things
are the same as they've always been? What if we're
just hiding together?"

Clawdeen ignored her. "Forget it, ghoul. You've
got this election in the bag." She tossed the pin

away—which landed in one of Frankie's bubbling beakers.

"Hey!" shouted Frankie.

The pin was sucked up into a coiled tubing. It got stuck. It blocked the experiment. The test tubes all started rattling. Smoke filled the room. The ghouls grabbed their safety goggles. *BOOM!* The experiment exploded.

All it took was one mistake for everything to go wrong.

Moanica and her Zomboyz were not acting like students. They sauntered into Dracula's Humanology class and took seats across from Draculaura and Frankie.

Dracula began his lecture. "Now, as we all know, humans can be quite curious creatures." He clicked a button, and projected on a screen was a photograph of an adorable kitten hanging from a tree. "A disproportionate part of their day is spent looking at cat pictures, like this one and this one." He clicked a button to show another photo—a cat dressed up as a burrito. "But while they portray this feline as a burrito, they have no plans to actually eat it."

Draculaura sighed with relief. Gob pounded on his desk. He wanted to eat everything.

"Can anyone tell me why?" Dracula asked the class.

Draculaura raised her hand. "Perhaps because they're vegetarians like me," she suggested.

"That's one guess," answered Dracula. "Anyone else?"

Moanica's hand was raised. "I have a question."

"Yes?" answered Dracula.

"Why do we care?" She smiled. The Zomboyz laughed mindlessly.

Even worse, some of the other Monster High students chuckled and smiled. This upset Draculaura. She stood up at her desk. "We might want to live among humans someday! It's important that we understand them!"

"Humans?" sneered Moanica. "Why don't we just eliminate them? It's a whole lot easier than groveling at their feet to make peace, don't you think?"

The class roared with laughter.

"Easier? Perhaps. But the easy way isn't always the best way. Or the right way." said Dracula.

The bell rang.

As Moanica sauntered out of the room, ghouls and guys clustered close to her.

"I hope my dad's right," worried Draculaura. "Because this election is not going to be easy."

Chapter 14

Zombie vs. Vampire

Gob scuttled toward the vending machine. But someone had covered it with chains and padlocks. There was no way for him to sneak more snacks. He shook the vending machine in frustration.

Someone was standing right behind him. Someone was whispering in his ear. "Who cares about consequences? It's better to take what you want than ask permission. The humans have all the snacks you could ever desire." Moanica was luring Gob out the front door of Monster High.

"Right down the road," she told him as she

pushed him down the front steps. She laughed to herself. This was going to be fun.

Later in the day, Draculaura stood on those same steps, getting ready for a debate with Moanica. She approached the podium. She looked out at a sea of faces.

Her father introduced the candidates. "First up, running for copresidents, the incredible founders of Monster High. Please give a warm welcome to Draculaura and Frankie Stein!"

The students stomped and clapped, roared and cheered. The Zomboyz booed. Clawdeen turned around and bared her teeth, growling.

Draculaura tapped the mic. She cleared her throat. "My fellow monsters. It seems like just yesterday that this building was just an old abandoned house, one that my dad and I worked hard to make a home. But it wasn't until we created Monster High that I truly felt at home."

Frankie leaned close to the mic. "And now we want to bring that feeling to the entire world. If elected, we promise to bring monsters and humans closer together."

"With outreach programs and field trips and seminars and sports and all kinds of fun-ness that we can share!" added Draculaura. "You see, whether you're a Normie or a monster..."

"A creepy crawlie or a beastie..." Frankie smiled.

"A vote for Frankie and Drac is a vote for kindness..."

"And understanding!" Frankie finished for her.

"A vote for Frankie and Drac is a vote for monsters and Normies getting along together!" Draculaura was inspiring. Monsters in the crowd were nodding their heads in agreement.

"So if you've ever felt a little bit wacky..."

In the audience, Bonesy looked up.

"Or a little bit strange..."

Woolee nodded her tusks.

"Monster High is here for *you*!" exclaimed Frankie. "A place where what makes you weird is what makes you unique!"

Moanica stood up. "Impossible!"

Draculaura defended herself. "Not impossible. Just challenging."

There was polite applause from the students.

Dracula took the mic. "Our next candidate Moanica D'Kay…"

But before he could say anything else, Moanica had leaped onstage and grabbed the microphone out of his hands.

"Needs no introduction," she announced to the crowd. "I'm not gonna try to tell you some mumbo-jumbo dream about living side by side with humans. Let's get real. These ghouls claim it's all about coming out of hiding in the dark. If I'm elected, I'll make sure we never have to hide from the humans because they'll be hiding from *us*! Vote for Moanica. Vote for monster pride!"

"What's so great about a world where everyone is afraid of us?" wondered Draculaura out loud.

Moanica shook her head. "You just don't get it. You've never been out in the real world like I have. You're too busy loving the Normies from the safety of your room."

Moanica hopped off the stage, still holding

the microphone. "You think Normies are your friend?"

She was standing in front of Woolee.

"When was the last time you left Monster High?" asked Moanica.

Woolee wouldn't meet her eyes.

"Don't have an answer do you?" said Moanica.

"Cheap shot!" shouted Frankie. "She doesn't talk!"

"She doesn't have to," Moanica shot back. "None of you have left Monster Hill. Face it. You're all still in hiding. The only difference is now you're hiding together."

The Zomboyz began chuckling together, as if on cue.

Dracula was about to step in, when out of the corner of his eye, he saw Gob disappearing with the entire vending machine on his back. He ran after him.

Moanica was still talking into the microphone. "Humans don't wanna live peacefully with us. So you can believe me, or you can believe a Normie lover. Have you seen her bedroom?" She pointed at Draculaura. "It's practically a shrine to that

Normie pop star Tash. But something tells me that Drac's precious Tash doesn't share the love for us monsters."

"You don't even know her!" Draculaura was so upset.

"And you do?" countered Moanica. "You think that Normie's your friend? Prove it."

Draculaura's eyes widened. "What do you mean?"

"Get Tash to come to our dance," dared Moanica. "Prove that she won't take one look at your monster face and scream."

Draculaura surveyed the audience. More than a few students were now standing by the Zomboyz, wearing Moanica pins. Her followers were growing.

Moanica was facing down Draculaura. "Just one appearance, and I'll take myself out of the race."

Cleo was shaking her head. *No. No. No.* But Draculaura wasn't looking at her.

"Fine!" agreed Draculaura.

Chapter 15

Freak-Out

A tour bus rumbled down a deserted country road. Tash's face was emblazoned on the side of the bus.

Just after the bus had passed, Lagoona emerged from behind a boulder. She took off on a skateboard. She caught up to the back of the bus, grabbed hold of the fender, and hung on. She peered through the back window.

Tash was sitting alone. She was checking her phone.

Lagoona pulled out a coffin-shaped walkie-talkie. "The eagle is in the nest," she reported.

"I repeat. The eagle is in the nest. Over." She put the walkie-talkie back in her pocket and got ready for the game plan. "Now it's time for Operation: Bus Sabotage!" she whispered to herself.

Clawdeen transformed into a werewolf. She jumped into the middle of the road just ahead of the bus. She snarled. The bus screeched to a stop. It swerved. Frankie snuck over to the hood. Sparks blazed from the engine. The engine died. The tour bus door opened, and the driver and Tash's manager got out.

"Did you see that?" exclaimed the driver. "*Something* was on the road."

The manager was throwing up his hands. "The bus is busted? Do not tell me that bus is busted. We got a gig here, people!"

On the other side of the bus, Lagoona was hoisting Draculaura up to the window. "Quick," Cleo urged.

The manager was complaining. "Time is money—let's go. Let's go! What? What? Am I the only one being honest here?"

Draculaura looked through the bus window. Tash was still looking at her phone. Draculaura tapped on the window. Tash looked around. "What was that?"

"Um…it's a fan!" whispered Draculaura. "Your biggest actually."

At first, Tash didn't seem to see anyone, and then her eyes spotted Draculaura. She smiled. "You want an autograph?"

Draculaura couldn't believe it. "You would do that?"

"Of course." Tash smiled sweetly. She opened the window and stuck her head out. "Anything for my biggest—"

She stopped in midsentence. Draculaura's vampire fangs were glimmering in the moonlight.

Tash gasped. "Fangs? You are a…You've got to get out of here." Tash looked up and then back at Draculaura. She wasn't scared. In fact, she seemed almost apologetic.

"But, but—" Draculaura hadn't asked her about the dance.

"*Go*, I said!" ordered Tash. "Just *go!*"

"Please…" begged Draculaura.

"Go." Tash started to scream. She screamed at the top of her lungs. She kept on screaming.

Drac retreated.

Tash's manager came running back on to the bus. "Tash, what is going on?"

The ghouls scrambled away from the bus as fast as they could.

Except for Draculaura. She turned into a bat and perched on the top of the bus. She felt betrayed. Her idol was terrified of her. Maybe Moanica was right.

Chapter 16

Snack Attack

Moanica was entertaining the Zomboyz in the student lounge with jokes and gossip. "And then the humans ran away screaming," she said. "It was so funny."

The Zomboyz laughed. Because they had to. They were her minions.

The doors to the lounge swung open. Draculaura and the ghouls were back. Had they been successful? There was a hushed silence in the room.

"Well?" asked Moanica. "How'd it go? We're all *dyyyyying* to hear."

Draculaura was pale. She could hardly speak. "I…She…Tash," she stuttered.

Moanica pretended to understand what she was saying. "She's here?" she asked with fake surprise. "I can't wait to meet her. Tash! Big fan! Hello? Tash?"

Draculaura was defeated. She couldn't look at anyone.

Moanica mocked her. "Your precious Normie took one look at you and went running for the hills. Guess I won't be dropping out of the race after all."

Moanica clapped her hands, getting everyone's attention.

"You hear that everyone? The election is back on!"

Draculaura ran out of the

lounge toward her room. *Moanica is a horrible, no good, very bad, awful monster,* she thought. She threw herself into her coffin. The only problem was that Moanica was right. She *had* scared Tash. *Maybe monsters and humans weren't meant to live together. Maybe we are all just too different.*

The ghouls followed Draculaura out of the lounge, but Rayth stopped Clawdeen. She spun around as he grabbed her arm.

"What is it, Rayth?" she asked. "Now's not the best time."

Rayth seemed nervous. "Oh, I, um, was just wondering if you'd be at the Monster High ball."

"You really think the dance is gonna happen once Moanica's in charge?" Clawdeen couldn't believe what she was hearing.

"Guess I should cancel the chocolate goblin fountain." Cleo was so disappointed.

"She hasn't won yet," said Rayth.

It was true. All that night, the Monster High students hit the ballot box. The results wouldn't be known until the next day.

Still, Draculaura was pretty sure that she knew

what was going to happen. The ghouls tried to cheer her up, but it was no use.

"There's still a chance," said Clawdeen halfheartedly.

"Right," agreed Lagoona. "You never know."

Venus burst into Draculaura's room. "Ghouls, you've got to see this," she exclaimed.

They hurried to the lounge, where all the students were hovering around a giant TV screen. Dracula looked troubled. The monsters were watching a Normie news show.

Someone had vandalized a convenience store. All the cookies and snacks had been stolen. Slime covered the empty shelves. "Some disturbing news has hit our quiet village," announced a reporter. "Police have released this rather unusual sketch of the suspect."

On the screen flashed a roughed-out sketch of someone who looked almost exactly like Gob. If Gob were a human being.

"There seems to be an abundance of goo at the scene," the reporter continued. "Uh, if you have any information regarding the suspect, please contact the police."

Dracula turned off the television.

Moanica cackled. "Ha! Ha! Good job, Gob! Now that's what I call monster pride!"

"I knew opening this school was a bad idea," Dracula fretted. "Now we're in danger."

"What are you saying?" asked Cleo.

"As soon as they follow the trail, they'll end up here and expose us all. Monster High is done for."

Clawdeen couldn't believe it. "But this is my home. *Our* home! Together."

"I'm sorry, ghouls." Draculaura was close to tears. "This school was probably all just a stupid dream."

Gob, lurking in the back of the room, looked upset too. What had he done? *Oh no. Oh no.*

Chapter 17

The Results Are In!

Clawdeen flung open the curtains in Draculaura's room. Light poured in. All the ghouls jumped on to her coffin trying to wake her up.

"Draculaura!" shouted Clawdeen.

Draculaura shielded her eyes from the sunlight. "What are you doing?" she asked groggily. "What time is it?"

"Time to wake up," announced Cleo.

Even when Draculaura was dressed and ready, she still didn't understand why her friends had woken her up so early.

"Because, ghoul, a president's got work to do," explained Clawdeen.

Draculaura yawned. "Class doesn't start for another…President?"

"Well, copresident technically." Frankie grinned.

The student lounge was packed with staff and students. The room was decorated with pink and black and electric-blue balloons, Draculaura and Frankie's favorite colors. As the ghouls walked into the room, the crowd began to clap and cheer.

"But I don't get it," said Draculaura. "I thought the whole school voted for Moanica."

Cleo shook her head, laughing. "The students believe in *your* dream."

Moanica was scowling. The Zomboyz were imitating her. One angry Zomboy punched his fist into his palm.

Moanica wasn't going to just accept defeat. "Dreamers, all of them," she hissed to the Zomboyz. "It's time to wake them up." She snapped her fingers. The Zomboyz grunted and followed her right away, except for one who slugged down a last sip of coffee. Zombies love coffee!

Dracula made his way through the still-cheering crowd to his daughter. "Congratulations, Madame President!" He gave Draculaura a big hug. He turned to Frankie. "And Madame Copresident."

"I guess we better enjoy it while it lasts," sighed Draculaura. "Once the village police department finds out who robbed the convenience store, we're gonna have to say bye-bye to Monster High."

"I wouldn't worry about that," said Frankie confidently. "I think *somebody* has something to confess."

An embarrassed Gob shuffled over to Frankie and Draculaura.

"Gob returned everything he stole last night," Frankie explained.

Someone switched on the television, and it was true. All the snacks had been returned. Of course, everything was covered in a sticky green goo. But still.

"Breaking news," announced a reporter. "It appears that everything previously stolen in last night's robbery has been returned mostly unharmed."

Draculaura was relieved. "You returned everything?" she asked Gob. "I could hug you, except I'm wearing my favorite dress."

"We may be monsters," said Dracula sternly, "but we're still civilized. And Gob is still in trouble."

Gob looked down at this feet, ashamed. He reached into his tummy and pulled out a slimy apple. He handed it to Dracula.

To his credit, Dracula accepted the gift. He even took a bite of it. He smiled. Not bad!

Cleo stepped in. "We could have Gob work catering for the dance…as a punishment."

Gob seemed to love that idea! He nodded enthusiastically.

Draculaura's face lit up. She'd just realized something. "The school dance is back on. Yes! Nothing can stop us now."

Rayth smiled at Clawdeen. He'd had faith the dance would happen.

What he didn't know was that Moanica had led her Zomboyz to the outskirts of the village where they were waiting. They stepped into the road. Tash's tour bus screeched to a halt. Moanica stepped forward. "Who wants to go to a party?" she announced with an evil laugh.

Chapter 18

Attack of the Living Dead

There was only one thing better than a monster ball—getting ready for the monster ball. The ghouls were prepping in Draculaura's room. Clawdeen brought in a clothing rack filled with funky creepy-chic dresses. Draculaura had decorated with pink and black. Frankie had brought pink and black snacks.

"Hey, ghouls!" exclaimed Clawdeen. "Get ready to dance the fright away." She switched on some music and invited her friends to start trying on outfits.

But they really needed her fashion sense. Oh, did they ever!

She gave Frankie a different pair of boots, helped Cleo with her jewelry, and suggested a new hairstyle to Draculaura.

"Wow, Clawdeen, you look fangtastic," complimented Draculaura.

The werewolf blushed. *"Aroo!"* she howled. "I can't wait to show Rayth!"

"Rayth!" squealed the ghouls together. "He asked you to the dance?!"

"Well…" Clawdeen shrugged, remembering a moment in art class just the other day.

She'd been working on one of her fashion sketches when Rayth interrupted her. Startled, she yelped.

"Er, well, um, I was wondering…" stuttered Rayth.

"Are we going to Dancing the Fright Away together or not?" Clawdeen blurted out.

"What? Um?" Rayth ran in fingers through his hair. "Why, I'd love that."

"Great." Clawdeen grinned. "Now that that's settled, you can stop sneaking up on me."

"Okay!" agreed Rayth. "It's a date." He walked off, grinning.

Frankie looked at her clock. "We better get going."

"You think we'll get a good turnout?" Cleo wondered. "This is the first time I got to plan something for everyone else!"

When the ghouls entered the outdoor dance pavilion, they couldn't believe what an amazing job Cleo had done. Glimmering gold chandeliers floated between the trees. A fancy fountain bubbled with warm, liquid chocolate. There was a photo booth for couples to snap special photos of this special night.

Seeing Cleo arrive, Deuce headed over to the ghouls. "Really cool party," he complimented her. "You did such an awesome job!"

Cleo smiled. "I know," she said.

Deuce seemed shy. "There's a photo booth here. If you wanted to…maybe…?" he suggested.

Cleo rolled her eyes. "Fine," she said.

Outside the booth, the ghouls watched the photos shoot out of the machine. Deuce struck a pose, but Cleo looked bored. In the next one, Deuce was making rabbit ears behind Cleo. Cleo was pushing Deuce away in another. By the last one, she was laughing and Deuce was too.

The ghouls poured into the Spook Booth for a photobomb. How would they all fit in? But they did! It was the best shot of all.

The lunch lady was spinning turntables with her many tentacles. Monster High students were busting their moves. Dracula looked dapper in a brand-new all-white tux. He was beside the punch bowl keeping an eye on everything.

"Can I interest any of you ghouls in some poltergeist punch?" he asked.

"Great!" said Frankie.

"I want some!"

"I'm so thirsty."

"Looks delicious."

Clawdeen's mom joined the ghouls. "I wouldn't

mind some punch," she said softly.

Seeing her, Dracula turned red and dropped the cup he was holding. "Ah, I think I'm all out."

Clawdeen's mother smiled. "Well, let's go back inside and whip up another batch." She steered Dracula back toward the house.

Rayth noticed Clawdeen and ran over to her. He was wearing a purple bow tie. His mouth dropped open when he saw Clawdeen up close. "Wow!" he said.

Clawdeen tossed her mane of curls. "You're not gonna get all mush on me now, are you?"

But it was too late. Rayth was already smitten. "Wh-what?" he stammered. "Not mush. Not me."

Clawdeen laughed. "Good."

An engine roared from down the road. The sounds of honking drowned out the music. A tour bus careened onto the lawn. The door opened, and Moanica appeared, her narrow eyes taking in the party.

The Zomboyz emerged from the sunroof and crowded on to the top of the bus.

"I'm hurt," announced Moanica. "You've started the party without me! I even brought you a present." With a devilish smile on her face, she snapped her fingers. Some of the Zomboyz were dragging someone out of the bus. It was Tash!

Draculaura ran toward her idol, but a Zomboy stopped her.

Tash was struggling against the Zomboy who held her tight. "Let me go you…you…you monsters!"

Moanica pretended to be shocked. "You hear that, everyone?" she said to the crowd. "Monsters! Now you know once and for all what your beloved Normies think of you."

"What are you doing, Moanica?" Draculaura demanded to know.

Moanica and the Zomboyz dragged Tash to the punch table. "Drac, relax," sneered Moanica. "I just want her to understand us." She smiled. "Then I want her to become one of us." She wanted to turn Tash into a zombie!

The ghouls didn't know what to do. But Cleo noticed that the Skullette hanging around Drac's neck was glowing. Why? She looked at the Zomboyz all clustered close to Moanica. She looked back at the Skullette. She had an idea.

Moanica was flaunting her power. "Anything to say to your beloved Tash before she joins my army?" she asked Draculaura.

But before Draculaura could answer, Cleo grabbed her arm. She winked. She motioned toward the Skullette.

Draculaura understood the plan immediately. The other ghouls nodded. They did too!

Draculaura clutched the Skullette and held it out in front of her. The ghouls all grabbed on. Draculaura turned to Moanica. "Just one thing. *MOANICA. EXSTO MONSTRUM!*"

POOF!

The ghouls vanished. Where were they?

A crackling noise above her head made Moanica look up. The ghouls were in the air right above her. How had they done that? They were slamming down toward the punch table. They were between Moanica and Tash!

"We won't let you do this, Moanica!" shouted Draculaura.

"How are you going to stop me?" Moanica was furious. "There's five of you. I have an army!"

"And so do they!" It was Rayth! The entire student body was standing behind him. They were all ready to fight for Draculaura.

"We are better together," whispered Draculaura.

Gob grabbed a tray of cupcakes, gobbled them up, and held up the platter like a shield.

Moanica's fists were clenched. Her eyes were

narrowed. Her teeth were bared. She snapped her
fingers, and the Zomboyz staggered toward the
students.

Gob let loose a bloodcurdling war cry and led
the charge against the Zomboyz.

But the ghouls knew that they were really
outnumbered. They were going to have to do
something. But what? They jumped down and
entered the fight. Draculaura locked eyes with
Moanica. Draculaura knew she had to defend
Tash from the zombie leader.

As Moanica lunged toward them, Draculaura
turned into a bat. She dove toward Moanica's
head. She flapped her wings like crazy.

Gob was swinging his enormous belly back
and forth, knocking down Zomboyz left and
right. Marshall, the swamp monster, charged the
Zomboyz and stuck them with his thorny head.
Crystal generated ice chunks from the moisture in
the air and flung them like boulders. She zapped
others and turned them into ice directly.

Cleo wrapped up a Zomboy in bandages but
didn't see another one creeping up behind her.
Just in time, Deuce whipped off his shades and

turned him into stone. He put them back on again before smiling proudly at Cleo. But he didn't see another Zomboy sneaking up on him! With a giggle, Cleo swung a linen bandage like a lasso and brought him down. They could both save each other. What a team!

The lunch lady was hurling LPs from every one of her tentacles. She was a great shot! Every single one brought down a Zomboy. She even kept the music going at the same time. Maybe she had found something she was better at than cooking!

Running away from one Zomboy, Frankie collided with another. They tumbled into the Spook Booth. *Flash! Flash! Flash!* Frankie emerged, dusting off her hands triumphantly, and sent a bolt of electricity toward a Zomboy riding on Woolee's back. *Zap! Zap! Zap!* The finished photos flew out of the booth. *Bam! Powee! Zowie!* In each picture Frankie was blasting the Zomboy with another jolt of electricity.

A Zomboy ran past, chased by the pack of Wolf cubs. Toralei, a werecat, tripped a Zomboy and went back to filing her claws. Were the monsters winning? Zomboyz were lying in groaning piles all across the ground.

Draculaura was still flapping her wings as hard as she could to distract Moanica. Lagoona kickflipped her skateboard into her hands and swung it like a bat, taking out a huge row of Zomboyz marching toward her.

Clawdeen had turned into a wolf and was shaking a Zomboy by the belt like he was a bone. She flung him loose, and he soared up into the air and right over the school. She reached around to grab another Zomboy, and he shuffled away from her, whistling as if he wasn't involved in this fight in any way at all.

Bonesy pulled off his own skull and pitched it like a baseball at a straggling Zomboy. The Mousicorn danced through a series of lightning-fast kung fu kicks and brought down a bunch of

Zomboyz ten times bigger than she was. Woolee stampeded like a crazed elephant.

Draculaura was now emitting a supersonic screech. Moanica staggered back, grabbing her ears. Seeing her chance, Draculaura turned into a ghoul again. Moanica was disoriented and slammed into a pile of stacked folding chairs—which collapsed on top of her.

Oh no! Draculaura rushed over. "Moanica! Are you…"

The ghouls were cheering. Tash was smiling nervously. Other students came over shouting their congratulations. Draculaura had defeated Moanica!

But zombie ghouls don't go down that easily.

A hand reached through the chairs, a zombie crawled out. She wasn't done yet. She leaped though the air—right toward Tash. Moanica's fingers were outstretched. She was going to do it! She was going to turn Tash into a zombie!

But Moanica flew right through Tash…as if…

Tash was a ghost!

Chapter 19

A Surprise

"It's time to come clean," Tash said to everyone.

"I did not see that coming," Cleo whispered to Deuce.

Draculaura was the most surprised of anyone. "Tash?"

Tash shrugged. "Ari Hauntington actually. Yes, I'm a ghost. But since I have the power to solidify, I've been able to live in the human world."

"Back up," said Clawdeen. "If you're Ari, who is Tash?"

"Tash is just a personality I made up so I could finally fit in," explained the singer. "No one ever needed to know who I really was. Until now. I'm Ari."

Draculaura was beaming. "There is nothing wrong with who you are."

Moanica chose this moment to try to slip away.

Dracula was returning with a new bowl of punch. There were Zomboyz rubbing their heads everywhere he looked. There was a new ghost talking to his daughter. What was going on?

"Why are you being so nice to me?" Ari asked Draculaura. "After the way I treated you, you must hate me."

Frankie stepped in. "That's not what this school is about."

"I'm sorry," Ari apologized. "How can I ever make it up to you?"

Draculaura grinned. She had an idea. "Well, I was going to ask you to sing at this dance...."

"Consider it done!" Ari was thrilled!

Cleo was even more thrilled. "A rock star playing at our very first high school dance! Whoever planned this event is a creative genius."

Clawdeen held up her hands. "Not so fast. This isn't just some high school dance. It's Dancing the Fright Away." She pointed at Ari's Normie fashions. "Let's get this ghoul monsterfied!"

Clawdeen whisked Ari up to her room. Hair. Makeup. Clothes. Clawdeen was going to turn her into a poltergeist pop phenom!

Ari whirled around when she was done. Lilac-colored hair fell in waves down her back. She wore fangtastic platforms and a totes rad outfit styled with chains. She couldn't believe how great she looked! She twirled in front of the mirror.

"So do you like it?" asked Clawdeen.

A huge smile spread across Ari's face. "It's me! Come on, ghouls. It's showtime!"

Draculaura was still trying to take it all in. Tash wasn't some flawless celebrity leading a perfect life.

She was a monster who wanted to be accepted, just like any other ghoul. She was Ari. Draculaura held the door open for her—but Ari floated through the wall instead.

Back at the pavilion, Frankie and Draculaura hopped onstage.

Frankie grabbed the mic. "Mansters and ghouls of Monster High. As your first-ever student council copresidents, it is our pleasure to welcome…"

"A world wide celebrity!" exclaimed Draculaura. "Our new student and newly discovered ghost…Ari Hauntington!"

Ari took the mic. She scanned the cheering crowds filled with monsters and beasties. She smiled.

"I've never seen a better audience," she told the crowd. "I've written a song just for this occasion. So let me hear it, Monster High!"

What a voice Ari had! What a song she had to sing. She was happier than she'd ever been. She was more herself than she'd ever been. She'd worn so many different faces, but "the best face to be is me!" as she belted out.

The monsters stormed the dance floor. The beat was crazy! Frankie let sparks fly. Cleo danced like an Egyptian. Clawdeen and Rayth busted a move. Clawdeen's little brothers watched, giggling. They pretended to dance just like Clawdeen and Rayth and made kissy faces until Mrs. Wolf bared her fangs. Then they stopped immediately.

Gob entered the Spook Booth with his true love—a tray of donuts. *Flash! Flash! Flash!* He photographed himself eating them all. His mouth was covered in jelly.

Dracula was dancing, and Draculaura was trying not to laugh. But she couldn't help it. He was just too funny! She started imitating his weird dad moves, and he thought she was impressed.

Lagoona started a wave and helped carry Ari across the crowds while she finished her song. It was pretty easy. In fact, she floated just above their hands.

Draculaura had never been so happy. Not only was her favorite singer performing at her very first dance, but Monster High had survived. Monster High was here to stay.

Moanica had been watching everything. She

was lurking in the shadows near the trees. She was disgusted with Ari's performance. "Enjoy your fiesta party now. This isn't the last time you'll hear from me!" She snapped her fingers. "Come on, Zomboyz."

A few Zomboyz turned toward her. They were woozy. They were holding ice packs to their hurting heads. But most of the Zomboyz ignored her. They were dancing! They were enjoying themselves! They liked Monster High!

Draculaura knew that there was still a long way to go. Monsters still hadn't learned how to live with humans, and humans were still scared of monsters. But Draculaura had a feeling that the day would come when everyone would get along and dance together. Why not? They had the most talented monster ambassador the world had ever known—Ari Hauntington.

No wonder Draculaura had always liked her!

Chapter 20

Time to Stand Out

Draculaura and her father soared through the night sky. Draculaura was now an expert at turning into a bat and flying. When they passed the billboard advertising Tash's tour, Draculaura fluttered to a standstill.

The billboard showed Tash singing her new song, "If You're Tired of Trying to Fit In, It's Time to Stand Out." Ari looked as solid as any Normie, but she was decked out in Clawdeen's most clawesome style.

"Come on, Drac," called her father. "You know how I feel about distracted flying."

"Coming, Dad," answered Draculaura. She took one last look at the billboard. "Now that's what I call flawless."

That night, she sat down to make another post on her vlog. She had hundreds of followers these days. She smiled into the webcam. "Sure, the humans thought Tash's new look was just a costume. But for the first time in ages, monsters were truly coming out of the dark! Because as you know, it's not impossible. Just challenging."

Cleo, Clawdeen, Frankie, and Lagoona were tiptoeing up behind her. They were making faces into the camera. They were photobombing her vlog!

Draculaura whirled around, laughing. "Hey, I'm trying to impart words of wisdom here."

The ghouls' faces became very serious. For an instant. Then they cracked up laughing and started hurling pillows at Draculaura. A pillow hit the webcam, and the screen went black.

Pillow fight break!

None of the ghouls would ever be lonely again.

MONSTERS ARE BETTER TOGETHER!
BLU-RAY™ + DVD + DIGITAL HD
WELCOME TO MONSTER HIGH
THE ORIGIN STORY
WELCOME TO MONSTER HIGH
COMING TO BLU-RAY™, DVD & DIGITAL HD*
UNIVERSAL
Visit us at MonsterHigh.com
NOT RATED
©2016 Mattel. All Rights Reserved.
*Not all formats available in all territories. Redemption code subject to expiration. Visit NBCUcodes.com for details.
UNIVERSAL PICTURES HOME ENTERTAINMENT
©2016 Universal Studios. All Rights Reserved.